Death in Sedona

A Ben & Bob Adventure

Bob Haider

Published by Bob Haider, 2023.

This is a work of fiction. Similarities to real people, places, or events are entirely coincidental.

DEATH IN SEDONA

First edition. December 4, 2023.

Copyright © 2023 Bob Haider.

ISBN: 979-8230532224

Written by Bob Haider.

To my daughters Bonnie Leigh & Anne Marie

My grateful acknowledgement is extended to my dear friend Ben Cusomato for his contributions to this piece.

And my thanks to Glen and Barbara Armstrong for their inspiration and input for this story.

Prologue

A campfire flickered in the darkness. Against the backdrop of a star-studded sky in the Arizona desert, three college students camped just east of Bell Rock outside scenic Sedona.

From Arizona State University they drove up from Tempe, a mere 2 1/2-hour drive. They arrived mid-afternoon and they planned to spend this Friday night, and Saturday here before driving back after breakfast on Sunday.

"I sure am glad we bought that firewood before we left. It has really cooled off," said one of them.

"Yeah, that's what happens in the desert," said another.

"We should have enough wood for Saturday night too...at least I hope so."

"Keep drinking," said the third student. "You won't get any warmer but if you have enough beers, you won't care."

In a sudden rush of wind, reddened embers from the campfire spun into the air. Sand and dirt swirled upward as the wind spiraled the embers into the night sky in a rising, funnel-like fire.

"What the hell?!" said one of the boys, as he jumped up and covered his eyes with his hands.

"Dammit!" yelled another, as he spit bits of sand and dirt from his mouth. "Must be a damned jet!"

"It can't be a plane!" yelled the third member as he quickly brushed hot embers from his shirt and jeans. "Not that low! Besides, there's no sound! No engine! Just wind!"

"What the hell is it then!?" said one of the students who stumbled, fell and began to laugh. "Beer is kicking in," he said through his laughter.

"Maybe it's one of those desert whirlwinds."

"A dust devil," one replied with the correct name.

"Yeah," said the one who was still seated on the ground, "the kind that kick up sand and dirt and look like skinny tornadoes. We didn't see any today. Maybe this is one of those," he hiccupped from his beer consumption. "Yeah, it's one of those skinny tornadoes," he repeated, and hiccupped again.

Suddenly, one of the young men saw an image arise from the desert floor and loom up in the darkness. The whirlwind extinguished most of the campfire, and the young man peered into the darkness attempting to identify the shadowy figure.

The mysterious outline moved toward him, and as it neared, the young man's eyes widened in terror. He tried to shout to his friends but couldn't utter a sound as he stood petrified in terror.

Something sprang upon him.

Instantly, the creature's razor-sharp incisors punctured the young man's neck and burrowed deep into him. Blood spurted from the wound and the creature gorged on its prey.

Death for the other two students would come just as swiftly.

Chapter 1

One month later.

It was mid-afternoon when Bob was behind the wheel of the Land Rover while Ben occupied the passenger's seat. The duo was headed northeast on Arizona State Route 17 which then veered onto 179.

In an attempt to make conversation, Bob commented, "Hippos...that would be my choice."

"What's that?" Ben asked, not looking up, as he leafed through a report.

"If we couldn't come back as a human and we had to pick one animal to come back as in another life, it would be a Hippo for me. Nothin' messes with a Hippo."

"Hmm," said Ben, as he concentrated on several paragraphs of interest to him.

"Oh, by the way, I don't think I told you but I received a subpoena last week from an ex-girlfriend," said Bob, as he shook his head in disbelief.

"Hmm," Ben nodded focused on the report.

"It's supposedly regarding a breach of promise. That's a laugh! But I don't have a clue as to what it's really about. I mean I never proposed marriage and I was never anywhere near that serious about her. I didn't think she was serious either. We dated; that's all," said Bob, as he glanced at Ben and saw his partner completely engrossed in his reading. "Are you listening to me!?"

"Yeah, sure," said Ben, as he flipped a page in the report. "You were saying an ex-girlfriend is suing for custody of your penis."

"I said I got a subpoena!" Bob yelled, as he shook his head and glanced out his driver's side window. He had been driving for a couple of hours since they picked up their rental after their flight touched down in Phoenix.

Bob's line of sight returned to the road and out of the corner of his eye he saw Ben's shoulders heaving, his partner unable to repress his laughter, but Bob wouldn't acknowledge being the butt of Ben's amusement.

"Where are we heading, anyway?" Bob asked.

"North," Ben answered.

"I know that! But where are we going?"

"I'll tell you when we get there," Ben replied nonchalantly

"Oh, thanks ever so much, bastardo!"

"I'm not being evasive. I'm not sure exactly where we're going. We're gonna stop and camp in the desert somewhere up the road."

"What!? So, that's what you've got in that other bag you packed! You've got a tent in there, don't you?!"

"Yeah, it'll be fun," Ben smiled.

A scrunched up look crossed Bob's face as if he were in deep pain.

"What's the matter?" Ben asked. "It looks like you're constipated."

"You're not far off. You mean literally...we're going to be out in the desert...with no plumbing?" Bob asked.

"You'll be fine...as long as you don't squat over a cactus," Ben chuckled, and added, "or a scorpion or a rattle snake."

"Don't forget about Gila monsters!" Bob yelled. "Those suckers have grooved teeth on their bottom jaw. When they bite into you, they don't let go, and they literally chew the venom into you from those grooves in their teeth. They're an abomination; they're ugly as hell; and they live here in the Sonoran Desert!"

"Well, try to relax," Ben urged him.

"Relax!? Relax!? I'll never get any sleep. I'll be up all night on the lookout."

"The probability that we'll see any of them is...,"

"Probability?! Do you have any idea how many people die in the desert every year?"

"No," Ben answered nonchalantly, "can't say as I do."

"Well," Bob hesitated momentarily, and then continued, "it's...it's a lot."

"You're the scientist. You would certainly know better than me."

"You're darn right about that!"

"So, have you been working on anything lately?" Ben asked in an effort to change the subject.

"Of course, I'm always working on something. I'm always working on some project of my own, if I'm not preparing some gadget for you to be used on one of our assignments. Presently, I'm working on a non-addictive pain killer."

"That would be awesome," Ben replied seriously.

"Yeah, it would be great for the elderly especially because they have so much pain in their latter years from various ailments. But that's not all. I'm attempting to develop it without any side effects so people can drive when taking it."

"Pain meds without impairment...that would really be something. That's quite an endeavor. Good luck. I hope you can do it."

"Yeah, thanks," Bob replied, as he glanced in Ben's direction, and asked, "Hey, you mind if I take a glance at that report you're so engrossed in?"

"Yes, I mind. You're driving; keep your eyes on the road."

"What is it, a secret? I thought we were partners," Bob protested.

"It's nothing you'd be interested in," Ben commented nonchalantly.

"Try me," said Bob.

"Okay, if you must know, I've been reading about the migration patterns of North American...,"

"All right, all right, never mind."

"You did remember to pack the latest gismo I asked you to construct, didn't you?" Ben asked.

"You mean the SRN system? How could I forget with all the reminders you left me? That's why I was not able to progress very far with my non-addictive pain killer project. I was perfecting the SRN system."

"And did you perfect it as per my specifications?" Ben prodded him.

"Have I ever designed something for you that wasn't per your specifications? I'd say it's a good working model," he replied without bragging. "Yeah, yeah, it'll do the job. And don't call it a gismo. My gismos are scientific inventions."

Chapter 2

As the sun was now quite low in the sky, the golden-reddish rays of sunset illuminated the mountains in shades of radiant color.

"This part of the country...the desert...is truly striking," said Ben.

"Yeah," Bob acknowledged. "It took millions of years of ecological change to set down layers of sandstone under an area where once an ocean existed. Rust formed from iron deposits on the sandstone and voilà," Bob gestured with his arms and hands extended in front of him. "The picturesque red rocks are the products of that process."

"Hands on the wheel please," said Ben, who added, "Yes, the mountains are breathtaking."

"To the east us lay the Mogollon Plateau and to the west House Mountain, a dormant shield volcano."

"Shield volcano?" Ben asked.

"That's a gently sloping volcano. It gets its name from a shield...like a Roman soldier's shield. Take that shield and invert it to form a convex dome. Shield volcanos are actually quite massive as the lava that flows from them spreads out and travels a long way."

"Oh, okay. Too bad we're not here in the spring when the desert is in bloom. It's gorgeous then."

"Yeah," Bob agreed, "and think how much lovelier it would be viewing the landscape from a hotel window."

Ben handed Bob a Kleenex.

"What's this for?"

Ben pointed at Bob's face, and responded, "You've got quite a lot of sarcasm dripping from the side of your lip."

Bob tossed the Kleenex back toward Ben. "All I'm saying is the desert would be so much more pleasant if we don't camp in the middle of it."

"Yes, I gathered you felt that way."

"Just what kind of case are we working on this time?" Bob asked.

"Getting away from the city...smelling the fresh air...being out in nature...camping. What does it matter what kind of case it is?" Ben asked.

"Oh yeah, it'll be absolutely wonderful," he grumbled. "There's no plumbing...no showers...no refrigerator...no television and hell, there's no telling what kind of critters of the night we'll encounter. No, it doesn't matter at all what kind of case we're on," Bob grumbled.

"As a matter of fact," Ben began, "this looks like a good spot. Slow down and pull off the road here."

"Where are we?" Bob asked, as he slowed the rental car.

"Not far from Sedona."

"Oh, yeah, I see Bell Rock in the distance. I recognize it; it's just south of Sedona. Well, maybe we're not all that far from civilization. Sedona is a tourist attraction now, but it first started as an artists' colony. The mountains—-in the morning light—-are even more colorful. Would-be Rembrandts would come from all over the country to paint in and around Sedona."

"Yeah, I know," Ben nodded, "but I didn't know you knew. I'm impressed. Have you camped here before?"

"Good God no! I've never camped in my life, but I did some hiking around Sedona in my college days and I remember reading about the Harmonic Convergence in 1987."

"Oh yeah, I know about that," said Ben. "The earth was in danger and at risk of spinning off into space. Only the psychic efforts of people on earth would alleviate the situation and keep the earth in its present orbit. Supposedly, if enough people concentrated around the globe, a New Age would begin."

"And they can always say that it worked," Bob laughed heartily, "because the earth remained in orbit."

"I've sometimes wondered who believes in that stuff," Ben commented.

"I ran across a couple of women in college who believed that...said there was a vortex of energy around here.

"Not the type of women that you could see as the mother of your children one day?" Ben smiled.

"Oh, definitely not anyone you'd want to introduce to mom and dad. Anyway, the beauty of this area is alluring but it can be eerie too."

"What do you mean?"

"Just that you hear some strange noises in the desert," said Bob. "I mean, no joke, it can really sound weird out here."

"What kind of noises?" Ben inquired with an anticipatory smile.

"The wind howls through the cliffs," he paused, as he looked into the distance. "It can sometimes sound like an animal whining," said Bob turned the car off the highway. "And I'm not exaggerating. It sounds very real. And oh, there is the occasional desperate screeching of an animal being eaten alive by another."

As Bob continued off road, he slowed the Land Rover considerably as the uneven sandy desert surface bounced and jolted himself and Ben.

"You can stop here," Ben directed him.

Bob stopped but left the engine running with the headlights on as the last rays of sunlight now flickered along the horizon while night began to creep across the Arizona desert.

"Don't worry, if the boogey man comes, we can just high tail it into town," Ben shrugged, but seeing that Bob was not amused, he quickly added, "I thought we'd sleep a lot better a couple of miles away from the highway away from the road noise. So, what do you say? Want to make a campfire?"

Bob gazed into the darkness apprehensively.

"Let's look for some fire wood or whatever else we can find that'll burn," said Ben. "Good idea to leave the engine running and the lights on so the boogey man doesn't get us," he laughed, "but here's a flashlight for you in case you veer out of the light. You'll need it to find some wood in the dark."

Bob took the flashlight and the duo went in opposite directions picking up what they could find.

As Bob searched in the dark with nothing but the small flashlight, he became quite annoyed at the lack of firewood, and mumbled to himself, "This is going to take forever! I guess over the 'millions of years of ecological change' there never were any trees in this area," he muttered to himself.

Then as if pretending Ben was standing in front of him, he mockingly mimicked Ben's voice, "Of course, if there were any trees millions of years ago professor, they'd be petrified rocks by now. The Petrified Forest National Park and the Painted Desert are not far from here, you know," Ben would say.

Bob followed that with a response to the imaginary Ben, "Yeah, yeah, yeah." Bob was never inhibited when it came to talking to himself...regardless of whether people heard him or not.

"Damn, it's getting downright chilly," he muttered, as the Arizona desert was cooling considerably. Suddenly something slammed into Bob and he was knocked to the ground unconscious.

Ben had collected a fairly large number of sticks and was about ready to head back when he heard a blood-curdling scream. Ben dropped the load of sticks immediately and rushed toward the spot of the sound and heard a high-pitched whine. He immediately quickened his pace to a flat-out sprint.

Ben leapt over a six-foot cactus with the ease of an All-American hurdler, as he saw the glow from Bob's flashlight beyond the other side of the Land Rover. When Ben reached it, he opened the passenger's side door, flipped open the glove compartment, retrieved his Glock handgun and ran out the driver's side door. Incredibly, he did that all so quickly he barely broke his stride.

A creature's high-pitch whine echoed through the desert a third time, as Ben came upon the scene of Bob sprawled upon the desert floor while a hideous winged creature circled over him its sharp, elongated fangs glistening in the light of a rising moon.

As the creature circled lower toward Bob, Ben bolted toward it and sprang into the air literally jumping more than two feet higher than the Olympic high jump record, and he did so from the footing of a sandy desert in street clothes. Ben grabbed the creature in midair, closing his hands tightly around its spindly legs just above its razor-sharp claws.

The creature emitted another high-pitched scream from Ben's vice-like grip. As it struggled to free itself, the creature flapped its wings frantically, ascended higher, and then abruptly dove toward the sandy desert and ascended again. Ben tightened his grip to hold on as he flopped in whip-like action as the creature attempted to dislodge his grip.

As the creature ascended once again, Ben put one hand atop the other and scaled up the creature, pulling himself up the creature's legs.

While Ben climbed higher, the gargoyle-like abomination pecked at his hands, its sharp fangs slashing him. With one final heave, Ben pulled himself up onto the creature's back. Now the hideous beast couldn't reach Ben with its teeth.

Ben grabbed at one of its wings and pulled it with all his might.

The creature squealed in agony. Ben held the wing tightly and the creature, no longer able to fly with one wing immobilized by Ben's grip, plummeted toward the desert.

Ben's grip slipped and he slid down the length of the creature but managed to grab one of its legs just above a claw with his left hand, but the creature's other claw caught Ben in his right bicep and one of its talons embedded deep into his flesh.

Ben dangled in the air holding on but twisted his grip on the creature's leg and it emitted another high-pitched shriek of agony as it lurched wildly in the air.

Suddenly, Ben was in a free fall. Luckily, the creature was low in the sky and Ben fell only a dozen feet to the ground. As Ben hit the desert floor, he did a summersault to avoid serious injury.

As the frightened creature regained the use of its other wing, it flapped both wings ferociously as it sped away and disappeared into the night. Only when Ben got to his feet did he realize one of the monster's bloody talons was broken and partially embedded in his arm.

Chapter 3

Ben dusted himself off and quickly approached Bob, who was now conscious though groggy. "Are you alright?"

Bob moved his head slowly back and forth, "I think so. I caught a glimpse of something flying away. It must have hit me in the back of the head as it flew over me and knocked me down," as he touched the back of his head gingerly and then looked at the palm of his hand, and added, "Good, no blood. Didn't break the skin. How about you? Are you okay?" Bob asked.

"I think so," Ben answered, as he felt his arms, legs and patted his ribs. "Sore, but I don't believe anything is broken."

"Hey, your arm's bleeding," Bob noticed. "One of its talons is broken off and sticking out of your arm. I'll get the first aid kit," as he got up and began to move quickly toward their vehicle, raised a hand to his throbbing head and slowed his pace.

Ben glanced into the distance in the direction of the creature's escape in the hope of following its path but it was too dark to see if the creature had continued straight ahead on its escape or if it had veered off in another direction.

When Bob returned, he tended to Ben. "Grit your teeth; I've got to get this talon out of you. The fact that it was bent as a claw made it more difficult to remove but Bob finally got it out and bandaged Ben's arm.

"Thanks," Ben nodded.

As Bob returned various items to the first aid kit, he asked, "You want to tell me what this case is all about now?"

"Thing is," said Ben, still attempting to catch his breath after his ordeal with the creature, "I really did want to go camping one day," he chuckled, as they walked back toward the car. I guess now isn't the time though to be roughing it in the desert."

"No," Bob replied, "but are we on a case or is this some kind of bizarre vacation?"

"We're on a case and that thing we saw is what we're after."

"Good," Bob proclaimed, "I'm glad it's about that creature because at least I know what's going on now...though not much because I didn't get a real good look at it before I blacked out. And speaking of that creature...you could have given me a heads up, you know. I could have been killed!"

"Yeah, sorry about that," Ben acknowledged. "Since I was briefed on its size, it's grown considerably and I didn't think it would be out so quickly after sunset, but yeah, I should have told you."

"Hmm," Bob muttered in a disgruntled groan.

"Well, we'd better get going. We need to head into Sedona to report what we saw," said Ben.

With visions of running water, plumbing and a motel room, Bob responded in understatement, "I suppose that would be best."

With Ben's injured arm, Bob got behind the wheel, and commented, "Well, one good thing."

"What's that?"

"I won't have to ask again what our assignment entails."

Ben nodded, "Yeah, and that creature is ugly as hell."

"You got that right," Bob agreed.

Chapter 4

It took a while to pack up their gear and it was after 2 a.m. when they arrived in Sedona. As they headed down main street, there was next to no activity at this late hour. Bob saw a couple exiting a bar so he slowed and rolled down his window.

"Uh, excuse me."

The couple appeared startled, as he asked, "Can you tell me where the police station is located?"

The couple paused, looked at each other momentarily and then walked off at a brisk pace.

Bob shrugged, "Must be tourists from the East."

Ben looked up the address on his phone and directed Bob to turn onto Roadrunner Drive.

Bob glanced at Ben with an upturned brow.

"That's the name of the road, honest. I guess in Arizona they take being in the desert to a whole other level," said Ben, as he shook his head.

"Why didn't you just look up the police station for Sedona and click on directions?" Bob complained.

"Why? To annoy you, of course," said Ben, as he spotted the police station. "There it is."

Bob pulled into a parking spot in front and they exited the Land Rover.

As they entered, Bob saw a restroom, and said, "Excuse me for a minute."

Meanwhile, Ben walked toward the front desk where an officer was seated. His nametag read Peterson.

"Hello," said Ben.

The officer looked up and nodded, "Good evening, sir. What can I do for you?"

"My friend and I...,"

The officer looked past him.

"He's in the washroom. Anyway, we were out on the desert...,"

"Camping?"

"Yeah, we were setting up camp but before we even had time to...,"

"You're from out of town, right?"

"Yeah, we are. Anyway...,"

"Out of state, right?"

"Yeah, but, as I was saying...,"

"Where are you from exactly?"

"What does it matter where we are from?"

"You saw something," the officer smiled.

"Yeah," Ben nodded.

"It's the desert. It does things to people who aren't familiar with it. It sometimes scares the crap out of city folk. Hell, it creeps me out sometimes and I'm an Arizona native. Probably why your friend is in the washroom now," the officer chuckled.

Bob approached and nodded a silent hello to the officer at the desk.

"Officer Peterson here doesn't believe we saw anything. He thinks whatever we thought we saw was a trick of the desert. Evidently, the desert plays tricks on people who are from out of town...and especially those who are out of state."

"What?" Bob asked in surprise.

"Look, we need to see the person who is charge here tonight so we can show him this," said Ben, as he flipped a portion of the creature's broken talon onto the officer's desk.

"What the hell is this?" the officer asked as his eyes widened.

"Like I said, we saw something," said Ben, his voice conveying distinct agitation.

Officer Peterson glared at him.

"That's called evidence. It's a portion of a creature's talon that broke off in my arm," Ben gestured to his bandaged bicep.

As the officer eyed the broken talon, he said, "All right, you saw something. Look, we get a lot of people in here from...uh...well...the UFO crowds. They're all over the desert—-Arizona, Utah, New Mexico."

"Well, we're not tourists," said Ben, as he flashed his Federal Identification while Bob pulled out his I.D. as well.

While Officer Peterson gazed at their I.D.s, Ben held out his hand in a gesture for the officer to return the talon and then in as patient a voice as Ben could muster, he said, "We're not from any UFO organization and that claw is not from any alien, though it is monstrous."

"Hmm," Officer Peterson mused, as he handed the talon back to Ben.

Ben leaned in, gestured with his forefinger for Officer Peterson to lean in closer as well, and said, "You get more than your share of UFO wackos here, don't you?"

Officer Peterson nodded repeatedly, "You can say that again."

"And you get those New Age folks, some of them on the fringe, who want to experience the power of the swirling energy vortex they claim Sedona is noted for."

"Oh, those people," he shook his head, "Yeah we get plenty of them here too."

"My point is...don't let your skepticism about those folks and their beliefs blind you to actual facts when they are staring you in the face," said Ben, as he dangled the talon in front of the officer.

Officer Peterson's unease was palpable as he said, "I'll get the Chief."

Chapter 5

"You guys can have a seat over there," said Officer Peterson. "Can I get you anything? Coffee? Water?"

"I would appreciate some coffee," Bob replied.

"Water for me, thanks," said Ben.

"Coming right up," he said, as he turned to head to the back, stopped and turned back toward them. "Hey, since you are both agents," he gestured with a nod of his head, "come on back to the lunch room. You'll be more comfortable there while you're waiting," a gesture he hoped would make amends.

"Yeah, sure, thanks," they both responded.

As the officer led them back to the lunchroom, he directed them to some chairs. "Have a seat. I'll get those drinks for you," as he moved to the coffee pot, poured a cup, retrieved a bottle of water from the fridge and brought them over. "You want any creamer or sugar?" he asked Bob.

"No, black is just fine."

"Donuts? They're not stale from the morning shift. They're fresh. The Chief brings them in fresh every night when he comes on duty."

"Maybe a bit later," said Ben.

Chief Bill Schmidt entered the break room and introduced himself to Ben and Bob, "I'm the police chief here."

"Nice to meet you Chief Schmidt," Ben shook his hand, as Bob echoed the same in kind.

"Now...uh...exactly what kind of Federal Agents are you?" the Chief asked.

"The temporary kind," Ben answered, as they each showed their I.D. "We're on special assignment...tracking the owner of this," said Ben, as he handed him the partial talon.

"Yeah, Peterson filled me in," as he held the talon, and examined it. "I'll tell you this talon isn't like anything I've seen. I mean it certainly is big."

"And we also want to report that we saw the owner of that," Bob piped in, "and Ben saw it more close up than he would have liked."

"Where did you see it?"

"Just southeast of Sedona," said Ben.

"Show me," said the Chief, as he gestured toward a map on the wall.

Ben approached it, perused it momentarily, and pointed, "Right about here."

An upturned eyebrow from Chief Schmidt and something in the Chief's manner that Ben picked up on prompted Ben to ask, "What is it, Chief? Something happen there?"

"Yeah, we received a missing person's report...actually three missing persons, a month ago...students from Arizona State University. Their fraternity said they came up this way for the weekend and never came back. They were camping in the same general area where you had your encounter with the owner of this claw," as he handed it back to Ben. "All we found was a dead campfire and their auto. There was no trace of them. We took samples of the sand near and around the area and the lab said there was blood in the sand," the Chief paused, looked at the clock on the wall, and added, "Fortunately, there's not a whole lot of policing that needs to be done in Sedona so I'm available now. We can head out there. Have a look see in the desert where you got this."

"It's pretty dark out there, Chief," said Bob.

"We're actually a real modern police department. In Sedona we have things like floodlights...searchlights. We can light that area up like it were day time."

Bob nodded awkwardly.

"Say, Chief," Ben began, "if this talon is from what I think it is, we're going to need to locate its habitat...which would be the caves in and around Sedona. Do you know of anyone who is acquainted with the caves in the area?"

"As a matter of fact, I do," the sheriff nodded repeatedly. "I know just the guy; he's a friend of mine; he takes folks on hikes...and on tours of caves around Sedona...and his house happens to be on the way to where you were attacked. We can stop and ask him if he'll be available."

Ben replied, "Sounds like exactly who we need, but...," Ben paused as he glanced at the clock on the wall, saw it was close to 4:30 a.m. and looked back at the Chief.

"Oh, don't worry," the Chief chuckled, "he and his wife will both be up. They arise a full hour before sunrise every day."

"Why?" Bob asked surprised.

"Come on, I'll tell you on the way."

Chapter 6

Chief Schmidt directed them to his Land Rover and the three of them got in.

"Nice wheels you have here," Ben commented.

"Yeah, one of these is a must here. You've got to have one for the desert terrain. Can't tell you the number of times I've had to go off road."

As they got underway, the Chief said, "Glen Armstrong is who we're going to see. He is a Canadian. He and Barbara, that's his wife, live here part time in the winters. Came here, gosh, I think it's been at least twenty-five years ago. He's retired now but he still does some work for his company part time. Has a client whose company is headquartered in Phoenix and he consults for them from time to time. As a matter of fact, he and his lovely wife Barbara will no doubt invite us to have breakfast with them.

"I am a bit hungry," said Bob, "but...uh...shouldn't we give them some advance notice of our arrival...after all, it's still pitch dark."

"No need," the Chief smiled, "like I said, they'll be up. Every time I see them, and often that's with one or two of my officers, they always invite us in for a meal...for either breakfast, lunch or dinner...depending on what time of the day it is. Of course, we don't always take them up on that...but Barbara is a great cook and Glen loves to grill...steaks, brats, chicken, salmon, you name it and he's good at it. My wife and I were on a vacation some years back and actually met them on a cruise, a river cruise in France...actually it was two river cruises combined into one. Anyway, at that time of year, September it was, they were still in Canada, they live about an hour's drive outside Toronto, and we got to talking and Glen tells me they winter every year in Sedona, Arizona where they have a place. I start chuckling and of course he wonders why I'm laughing and I tell him I'm the police chief in Sedona. Well, we were friends instantly and that's saying something because I don't readily make friends. And my wife and Barbara hit it off like sisters and they became friends straightaway as well. Yeah, my wife and I have been to their place many times for dinner over the years and vice versa."

It was only a twenty-minute drive to the Armstrong's and it was Barbara who went to the door when she heard a car pull into their driveway.

When Barbara opened the front door and saw Chief Schmidt with two others, she yelled back at Glen in the kitchen, "We have company. Put sausages and eggs on for five of us."

"Okay," came a response, as Glen had just flicked the switch on the coffee maker.

"Hi, Bill," she greeted him.

"Hi, Barbara. This is Ben and Bob. They're in town concerning an investigation."

"Oh? Well, hello, gentlemen. Come right in."

"I hope we're not imposing," said Bob awkwardly.

"Not at all; we were already up and breakfast is being prepared for the five of us so I hope you're hungry...sausage and eggs," she beamed.

Ben and Bob both nodded, and answered, in unison, "Oh, sounds good."

"Who doesn't like pork sausage?" Bob asked rhetorically.

"Well, come on in and have a seat. Glen is on breakfast duty this morning but I'll go spell him so you can be introduced," as Barbara retreated to the kitchen.

When the mustached Glen Armstrong entered the living room, the Chief made the introductions, and Glen chuckled, "Good timing, gentlemen."

"Sorry to pop in on you like this unannounced," Ben said.

"No, no, glad to have you. Besides, if Chief Schmidt brought you by, then I know it's important."

Barbara began setting the dining room table for five, and Glen asked, "Can I help with anything hon?"

"No, I'm good. Sausages are cooking so I can step away to do this. No problem."

"Okay."

It was the Chief who began. "Ben and Bob are on an assignment...uh...an investigation and they have something I thought you might want to see because they are going to need a guide."

The Chief glanced toward Ben, and said, "Show him what you've got."

Ben handed Glen the broken talon for his examination. While he examined the partial talon he asked, "Where'd you get this?"

"From my arm," Ben grinned, "the creature who owns it broke it off there."

Glen shook his head, and commented, "Ow, that must have hurt."

Ben nodded his acknowledgment.

Glen studied the talon and finally ventured, "I've never seen anything like this...I mean a talon this size...it must have come from a creature eight feet tall."

"Ten," Bob stated unequivocally. As Ben looked at Bob in surprise, Bob added, "I believe I got a fairly good glimpse of it before I went unconscious."

Barbara entered to announce. "Breakfast is on the table," as they all arose and moved into the dining room.

"Gentlemen, if you would both be seated there," Barbara gestured to a pair of chairs on one side of the table for Ben and Bob, as the Chief sat at one head of the table, Glen at the other, and Barbara opposite the agents.

"This is a god send," Bob commented, "you being up at this hour and it is so nice of you to serve us breakfast."

"No trouble at all," Barbara smiled.

"We're always up at this time," Glen stated, and added, "Early tee times with my group."

After they enjoyed the sausage patties, scrambled eggs and were sipping their coffee, Glen examined the talon again. "How many creatures did you see?"

"Just the one," Ben answered.

"How many do you think there are?" Glen asked.

Bob responded with a shake of his head, "We won't know for sure until we locate them but we believe it's a small colony."

"So, if they're ten feet tall why hasn't anyone seen them?" Glen scoffed.

"They hunt at night," Bob answered.

"And we believe they've only recently arrived," Ben added.

"Well, where'd they come from?" Glen asked.

"At the present time we don't know that either but we're backtracking their point of origin," said Bob.

Glen returned his attention to the talon, and mused, "Well, if this is what I think it is, you are correct. You're going to need a guide to the caves to find the owner of this talon...and all its brothers and sisters. The caves that would accommodate the size of the owner of this talon...," his voice trailed off as he considered the possibilities.

"Yes," Ben confirmed, "we'll need a guide who knows the area and can tell us which caves are large enough to accommodate these creatures."

Bob looked toward Ben and gestured awkwardly with an upturned eyebrow toward his partner hoping that Ben would avoid suggesting the elderly Mr. Armstrong.

"Hmm, well, there are several caves that are possibilities," Glen stated. "I'll give it some thought because not all of the caves would be large enough...some are not even caves...more like an indent in the rock like The Birthing Cave. It got its name when the Hopi people sent their pregnant women there to give to birth."

"Why'd they send them there, anywhere?" Bob asked.

"That's something I don't know, but though it's too small for your purposes, The Birthing Cave is great for hikers because it has elevation and there is a very scenic view which makes for great photographs. There are other, larger caves though. I'll think about it and get a list together. Yeah, you'll certainly need a guide. Sure, I can do that for you. Been in and out of those caves and others dozens of times. Yeah, I'll guide you," as he glanced toward Chief Schmidt, and continued, "I'm fully booked this week but I'll cancel any and everything in a heartbeat whenever you give me the word. Just let me know when."

The Chief nodded, while Bob squirmed a bit in his chair and Ben knew exactly what Bob was thinking regarding the white-haired, half bald, Glen Armstrong.

As nothing escaped Barbara's attention, she asked, "Is everything okay, Bob? You seem a bit nervous."

"Uh...anticipatory anxiety. It's a condition. I worry...ahead of time."

"Hmm, anticipatory anxiety...never heard of that," said Barbara.

It was Ben who offered an explanation, "Oh, it's like going out to dinner, turning into a parking lot, and commenting, "Oh, it's gonna be difficult turning left out of here when we leave."

"Ahh," Barbara responded in recognition, "now I understand."

"Yeah, he worries about everything, but it does have its good side because he pays attention to detail and nothing escapes his scrutiny. That comes in handy in our line of work."

"You all do know I'm in the room, right?" Bob scoffed.

Ben grinned, and continued, "Getting back to the matter at hand...yes, we're going to need to search the possible habitats of the creatures...any and all caves big enough within fifty miles of here."

"A tall order," stated Bob to emphasize the enormity of the undertaking.

"I'm sure the terrain will be quite challenging," said Ben, as Bob again glanced awkwardly at Ben.

Ben hesitated momentarily, but added, "Well, actually, we only need you to make a list of those that would be large enough. GPS can get us to the caves," he emphasized. "We don't expect you to actually take us into them."

"You have to enter if you expect to...,"

"We would certainly enter," Ben interjected, "but we wouldn't expect...uh...," Ben's voice trailed off.

"Oh, I see. You think I'm too old. Is that it?" Glen prodded him, "You think I'm not up to it."

"Well, no offense but...,"

Barbara's steely blue eyes sparkled while she attempted to suppress a grin as she knew what was coming and would thoroughly enjoy the upcoming scene as it unfolded.

Glen extended his arms and placed his hands, palms down, on the dining room table. It was the body language that foreshadowed someone about to arise from his chair, lean over the table and commence a heated rant to those seated for breakfast.

Belying that gesture, the soft-spoken Glen Armstrong calmly began to elaborate while Barbara's grin grew wider. "I golf three days a week...18 holes each time. I don't take a cart. I walk the entire golf course. Another three days a week and sometimes four, I conduct hiking tours in and around Sedona, and, yes, into the caves to guide folks as the caves can be treacherous in spots for those unfamiliar with them."

"We meant no...," Bob attempted to interject.

"On the hot days, I do this early in the morning at the break of dawn before the stifling heat. I walk fully...at a minimum mind you...50 miles per week, every week! So, let me ask you, gentlemen. How many miles do you walk every week? Hmm?" as his eyes darted back and forth from Ben to Bob and back again.

There was an awkward silence as Chief Schmidt having taken all of this in with subtle amusement attempted to stifle a grin while Barbara's grin moved into a full-blown smile, as she asked, "More coffee anyone?"

Chapter 7

"Mayday, Mayday, this is Phalanx one...two...seven. Mayday," called the pilot.

"Come in Phalanx one...two...seven. This is Sedona Oak Creek Airport Authority. Over," a voice responded calmly but with concern.

"I'm heading due south at 150 mph!" he yelled. "I've got engine trouble and losing altitude quickly. Do you have me on radar? Over," said the pilot.

"Negative Phalanx one...two...seven. This is a non-towered airport. Please provide your position and heading. Over."

"Holy crap!" screamed the pilot. "We're going down!"

"Come in Phalanx one...two...seven! Do you read!? Over."

Only static was heard from the radio.

"Phalanx one...two...seven do you read!? Do you read!? Over."

A call was immediately placed to search and rescue and another to the F.A.A.

Chapter 8

When Chief Schmidt was contacted by the radio dispatcher, he answered immediately, "Yeah, Susan?"

"We just got notified a small plane went down. The flight plan shows there was a pilot and one passenger."

"When it rains, it pours."

"Say again, Chief?"

"Uh, nothing, Susan. Contact search and rescue."

"They've already been contacted, Chief."

"Okay, good. Whereabouts did it go down?"

"They don't have a specific location...east of Sedona is the best they could advise and they can't even say how far east."

"Well, that certainly isn't much to go on," the Chief muttered. "Contact Billy and send him east with a team. Tell him to keep going east. Hopefully, the pilot landed safely but if it did crash there could be flames and they'll be seen in the dark. When the copter gets in the air, they'll have that high-powered searchlight. In any case, keep me posted."

"In the meantime, we're going to go have another look see near where those three college kids disappeared."

"Roger, Chief."

"Over and out," said Chief Schmidt, as he turned to Ben, and said, "How about you showing me exactly where you plucked in the arm with that talon?"

"Not a problem," said Ben.

The Chief turned back to his host and hostess, "Barbara and Glen, "Sorry we have to run."

"We understand," they replied in unison.

"Thank you so much for breakfast," which was echoed by Ben and Bob.

Barbara replied, "You're most welcome. Hope everything turns out okay with that plane."

Chapter 9

When the trio arrived at the scene, Bob asked, "We're not going to split up in the dark, are we?"

The Chief eyed the duo curiously, and asked, "Are you fellows armed?"

"Yeah," Ben answered, as he had previously handed Bob his gun. "We have one handgun between us."

Though Bob was quite familiar with firearms of all types, he pulled out the Glock, hefted it in his hand, and commented, "It somehow seems rather inadequate considering the size of that creature. Do you have anything larger Chief...something along the lines of a grenade launcher perhaps?"

"The Glock will do just fine," Ben interjected.

Chief Schmidt's eyebrow upturned, "You two better stick with me. Come along then," the Chief gestured with a tilt of his head and the trio exited the car.

"So, you don't have your own individual issue of firearms?" The Chief asked curiously.

"We're not those kinds of agents," said Ben ambiguously.

"Oh, you're what they call a special agent then," the Chief commented.

"The F.B.I. has a designation of Special Agents. We're more like unique agents," said Ben without offering specifics.

"Oh," the Chief responded with uncertainty, while he understood the agents weren't going to tell him anything further. Over the years he'd dealt with a few federal agents and found them to be secretive as well.

"The creature is nocturnal," said Ben, "so we'd best keep our eyes peeled."

When the Chief's countenance expressed surprise, Ben postulated, "just saying it attacked us at night, so it's out after sunset...it's nocturnal."

"Hmm," Chief Schmidt muttered.

"So, how are we going to do this?" Bob asked.

"We're going to canvass the area together, and we'll move in concentric circles ever widening out from our vehicle," the Chief explained.

Ben understood the Chief was being cautious in not wanting them to split up though it would have permitted the trio to cover more ground more quickly.

"I've only got two flashlights, so the three of us will walk abreast," as he handed one of the flashlights to Ben. "The two on the outside will scan the area with the flashlights as we walk."

"I guess that means I'm in the middle," Bob grumbled.

Just a couple of minutes after they got underway, Bob fell clumsily to the ground.

Ben reached out and assisted in getting him to his feet.

"You alright," asked the Chief.

As Bob dusted himself off, he complained, "It's that damn buffelgrass. I tripped over a clump of it."

"Yeah, this is going to be slow going," said Ben.

It was fifteen minutes later that Bob abruptly stopped in his tracks as dawn approached.

While the Chief and Ben were scanning their flashlights to the right and left of them, Bob was looking straight ahead, and he was the first to see the outline of it. He felt a lump rising in his throat but managed to find his voice, "Holy crap!"

The Chief and Ben quickly turned and looked at Bob and saw he was staring straight ahead. They turned their line of sight and aimed their flashlights straight ahead to see what had caught Bob's attention.

"Damn!" uttered the Chief, as he gazed in wide-eyed disbelief at a creature he had never seen the likes of before. It was crouched over a coyote that was alive but disabled and the creature didn't seem to mind the approach of visitors.

"What the hell?" Chief Schmidt voiced his dread, as he reached for his weapon.

Ben gently placed his hand on the Chief's arm, and cautioned in a whisper, "Careful, there could be others in the vicinity and we don't want to alert them. They don't attack in mass but they don't travel solo either and we already know they're aggressive. Let's not take a chance."

The Chief was taken aback but he understood and as he stared at the creature before him, he asked, "What in God's name is it?"

"Diphylla ecaudata," Bob responded.

"What?" the Chief asked without turning his gaze away from what was in front of him.

"A hairy-legged vampire bat," Bob stated matter-of-factly and without hesitation, "as opposed to Desmodus rotundus which is the common vampire bat, or Diaemus youngi, the white-winged vampire bat respectively.

Ben nodded, "I didn't know its scientific name but...yeah...that sounds about right. It's a bat."

"A bat!?" the Chief replied incredulously. "It's huge!" he said, as he eyed the creature hunched over its prey."

"It's feeding," said Bob, as the trio stood riveted upon the scene before them.

"Let's just all back away, slowly...and very quietly...to the Land Rover," Ben directed them.

"I can't just leave that monstrous thing out here to attack people," Chief Schmidt whispered, as he began to raise his weapon.

Ben once again placed his hand on the Chief's arm, shook his head repeatedly, and raised a finger to his mouth to be very quiet.

Slowly, the three of them moved away and returned to the Chief's vehicle and got in.

"I sure as hell hope you're right about me not obliterating that monster."

"Ben is right," said Bob, as he scooted a bit forward in his seat in the back, and continued. "There are most definitely more of them and if we had alerted them to our presence, I have no doubt they would have attacked us.

"That...thing...if it was feeding, it wasn't acting like any vampire bat!" the Chief declared.

"Contrary to the mythical vampires of the movies," Bob began, "vampire bats don't suck blood from their victims. Oh, they hone in on an artery for a hardy meal alright, but they make an incision with their razor-sharp front teeth, then lap up the blood with their tongue. The bat has proteins in its saliva that act as painkillers and their victims don't feel any pain. Additionally, the proteins also act as anticoagulants which keep the blood flowing."

"That's gross," the Chief commented, "but the size of it. It's huge," the Chief repeated. "How did it get so big?"

"We don't know, Chief," Ben answered.

Chief Schmidt started the engine and placed a call to the dispatcher. "Susan, we're heading east to see if we can see any sign of where that plane went down."

"Roger, Chief."

The Chief shook his head, and muttered, "It's turning out to be quite a night," as light began to peak above the horizon.

As they got underway, "Chief, come in, Chief," came over the radio.

The Chief grabbed his radio, "I hear you, Billy."

"Just checking in to let you know I'm on the road."

"Good. Keep your eyes peeled."

"You got a team out there with you, Chief?"

The Chief smiled, "Yeah, I've teamed up with a couple of federal agents."

"Come again?"

"Just let me know if you spot anything at all, Billy. We are on our way to the crash area as well."

"That's a Roger."
"Okay. Over and out."

Chapter 10

"Chief, come in."

"Yeah, Billy," Chief Schmidt replied.

"I went east out of Sedona about seven miles up to Schnebly Hill Vista. As the sun was rising, I scanned the surrounding area with the binocs. I got a good look and spotted a glimmer of something reflecting off a metallic object. It was the plane alright just past where the 801 connects with Schnebly Hill Road. I got over there and saw the pilot brought it down in one piece. There wasn't any evidence of any explosion or fire, but there wasn't a sign of anyone either."

"Okay. We're on our way. Watch yourself."

"What's that Chief?"

"We believe there's some creature creeping around in the desert, and it's serious, believe me, so take heed what I said. That's an order."

"Oh, okay, I'll be careful. I won't get out until I see you pull up."

After the Chief disconnected, Ben said, "Sounds like a good man you have there, Chief."

"When we're on duty, he's very formal and insists on addressing me by my title. Yeah, his mother raised a good kid in Billy, Junior," said the Chief proudly.

"Your son," Ben smiled.

"Yeah, I used to tell him it's okay to call me dad while we're on duty but he'd have none of that so eventually I gave up. He likes to keep it official."

"It must be nice...father and son working together. So, if you don't mind me asking, how come as the Chief you work the night shift?"

"Not much crime in Sedona but would you believe I thought it would be even all the more peaceful taking the night shift?"

Ben grinned.

"Anyway, Mrs. Schmidt gets a good night's sleep and I'm not one that has to go somewhere to wind down like those tv police shows. No, I go straight home, hit the sack and sleep like a baby. We have the afternoons and our evenings together and that seems to work for us. But I guess that's more info than you...,"

"No, no. That's okay Chief."

"Hey, there's Billy's van," said the Chief. He turned off the road, maneuvered to avoid a Saguaro cactus and weaved his way to the police van that Billy had driven.

The trio got out of the vehicle and saw a helicopter approaching in the distance.

Billy was standing beside the crashed plane, and had a flare going, as the Chief neared, and shouted, "I told you to stay inside!" Chief Schmidt's eyes flashed in anger that Billy had exited his vehicle.

"It's okay. I've been careful."

When the Chief saw his son eying the others, he said, "This is Ben and Bob. Agents, this is Officer Billy Schmidt."

Ben asked, "What's the story here?"

"Pilot got the plane down and it skidded to here. No crash and no fire but no one on board. I checked the radio but it's damaged. I guess they figured it was better to walk toward Sedona than to stay put since they couldn't contact anyone."

"Or they were frightened away from the plane."

Ben scanned the immediate vicinity, and said, "Look, the survivors had begun to set up a small campfire."

"Yeah," Billy agreed, "and I found some tracks before you arrived. They head off in that direction," he gestured."

Ben put his hand over the embers, "Still warm," he announced. "They're probably not far."

"Something caused them to move away from here," Bob ventured.

"Yeah," Ben nodded his agreement, "and we know what."

"What?" Billy asked, but when he didn't get an answer, he said, "I notified search and rescue that I found the plane and notified them that no one was here but that I found footprints from the pilot and passenger.

I gave them the direction they were headed, and lit a flare to signal them from where to begin the search."

"Good, good," said the Chief. "Hopefully, they'll find them soon."

"I also informed them about what you said regarding a creature in the desert. After they finished laughing, I informed them that the information was coming directly from the Chief of Police."

"That's good. They need to be on the lookout for a very large bat," said the Chief.

"A bat!?" Billy repeated incredulously. "What do you mean a large bat?"

While Chief Schmidt informed Billy what they knew regarding the creature, Ben made a cursory examination of the plane, and beckoned, "Bob, come have a look at this."

As Bob approached, Ben pointed to scratches on the outside of the pilot's door of the plane.

Bob eyed Ben with a confirming nod, "Yeah, those sure look like scratches from a claw alright."

"You know, other than the scratches, there's very little damage," Ben noted. "Not even a window is cracked."

And no sign of blood inside the plane."

Ben asked, "So, you said earlier your estimate of its size is ten feet tall?"

Bob exhaled deeply, "Well, I didn't use my instruments for measurements and I wasn't thinking very clearly at that point due to the blow to the back of my head...,"

"Yeah, yeah, duly noted," Ben interjected impatiently with a shake of his head as he was more than annoyed.

Bob replied quickly, "I'd say it was ten feet tall with a wing span of as much as sixteen to eighteen feet, and the wind displacement...my goodness, it was like one of those small helicopters built for one person."

"Agents!" yelled the Chief. "I found something. Come look at this!"

The duo moved quickly toward the Chief, as he gestured, "Take a look."

Ben and Bob stared intently at the sandy surface of a print, "It's from one of those creatures alright," said Ben.

"Yeah, at least one of those monstrous bats was here," said Bob, as a sudden wind hurled sand and dirt into the air.

"What the hell?" the Chief yelled.

Ben, Bob and Billy ducked their heads and covered their eyes.

Chief Schmidt pulled out his handkerchief and covered his face while Billy shouted, "Another one of our Sedona dust devils."

After the wind subsided, a look of concern showed on the Ben's face, as he yelled, "Get into the van! Everyone! Now!"

The urgency in Ben's voice conveyed the immediacy of the danger at hand and no one hesitated, nor did anyone look around to see what Ben was referring to, as the four of them ran to the van, hurriedly piled in and slammed the door.

Bob's eyes met Ben's, and Bob stated without a question in his voice as the Chief and Billy looked on, "You saw one of them."

Chapter 11

Inside the van, the group of four peered out the windows to see if they could catch a glimpse of the threat that lurked outside.

"What now?" the Chief asked.

"We wait," said Ben.

"Wait for what?" Billy asked.

He soon got his answer.

Just a few feet away an enormous, grotesque creature loomed up in the faint light.

"What the hell is that?!" Billy yelled, his eyes nearly popping out of their sockets.

"Yeah...that's pretty much everyone's reaction," Bob deadpanned.

Astonished, Billy couldn't turn his gaze away. "I thought you were exaggerating. That is one grotesque, giant, mother...," as his voice trailed off.

Billy started the engine and shifted into drive, when Bob yelled. "No! No! No! If you attempt to drive away it very well may attack."

The Chief, in the front passenger seat nodded to his son that Bob was correct as Billy paused and eased the gear shift into park.

Slowly, the creature approached the van and peered into the passenger's side window and observed the occupants inside.

"It studying us," Bob stated matter-of-factly.

"I thought bats navigated by radar and couldn't see," said Billy.

Bob couldn't take his eyes from the creature, as he answered, "Actually, several species of bats can see quite well with large, round eyes...just like the eyes of this monster."

"Oh, yeah? Well, those large eyes are staring at us...like it's scrutinizing us," the Chief snapped.

"It's probably considering what side dish to serve with us at dinner," Bob commented drolly.

The Chief, perturbed, did a slow turn and eyed Bob.

"Ignore him, Chief," Ben advised, "his sardonic sense of humor is on display at the most inappropriate times."

"Hmm," the Chief muttered, as the creature raised a claw, scratched at the door and let out an ear-piercing screech.

The Chief reached for his handgun in case it busted through the window. Regardless of the risk of a swarm of bats, the Chief was readying himself to shoot.

"That's the ugliest thing I've ever seen in my life!" said Billy.

"You may want to move away from that window, Chief. There's no doubt he could bust through that with no effort at all," Bob stated.

"I'm ahead of you on that score," said the Chief nervously, as he moved from the window and headed for the back of the van with Ben and Bob.

"If that creature can see, what's stopping it from attacking?" Billy asked, as he too moved to the back.

"It's sizing up the situation and may not know what to make of what it sees," Bob suggested. "It probably never saw a vehicle like this before, and on top of that...we're inside."

"Is that the same creature you battled?" the Chief asked.

"It's certainly the same kind of creature," Bob responded, and asked, "Did you notice if it had a broken talon, Chief?"

"Nah, my eyes were transfixed on its teeth."

"How the hell did it get so big?" Billy asked in stunned surprise, and repeated his question, "How did it get so damn big? It must be eight feet tall!"

"Yeah, people keep underestimating its height probably because it crouches but it's fully ten feet tall," said Bob, "and make no mistake, it's a bat all right."

"Look at the size of that torso!" Billy said in bewildered awe.

"So," the Chief began, "how did a bat get so damn big?"

"As I've stated...we don't know," Ben replied, "though that is part of what we are assigned to ascertain, if possible, to learn exactly what caused such massive growth, but our main objective is to locate them."

"Mutants," Bob added off the cuff.

"What's that?" the Chief asked.

"Mutants," Bob repeated. "Mutants are actually more common in nature than you might think," Bob noted.

"And no doubt there are plenty more of them," Ben added.

"Yeah, I think it's logical to assume there is a colony of them," said Bob.

"A colony of bats this size!" the Chief shook his head contemplating the possibility. "No one would be safe," as Chief Schmidt continued to grasp his handgun while pointing it at the creature.

"Don't shoot!" yelled Ben, "I don't think it's gonna try to get at us."

"What do you mean? You said he could shatter the windows!"

"If it was hungry," Bob interjected, "it's a good possibility one of us would already be dead."

Nevertheless, the Chief continued to level his gun at the creature, as it continued to claw tentatively at the outside of the van.

"Wait Chief," cautioned Bob, "it's clawing as a means to discover its surroundings. It's not attempting to get into the van."

"You're not one of those 'capture it alive so we can study it' types, are you?" the Chief asked facetiously.

Ben calmly said, "I'll remind you that a gunshot could signal many of the others. You don't want this creature's brothers and sisters alerted to make a smorgasbord of us, do you?"

The Chief paused, then relented and nodded in agreement, "Okay, but if it breaks that window, I'm blowing it away."

"You'll get no argument from us on that," said Ben.

The Chief then spoke into his radio. "Susan, come in, emergency. Come in."

The four occupants of the van continued to hear the sound of scratching claws against metal as if the creature was toying with them while all that separated them from it was the width of a glass window. As they watched, they hoped and prayed the creature would get bored and leave.

The sound of the dispatcher's voice came over the radio, "Come in, Chief."

"Sound the alarm!" the Chief instructed. "Get everyone inside!"

"What is it, Chief?"

"No time for questions. Just get everyone off the streets! It's an emergency. This is a dangerous situation and there is no time to waste. No one, absolutely no one, is to be allowed outside. Broadcast we have a police emergency. Everyone, no matter where they are, must shelter in place. Those on the road must stop and go inside. Use the storm siren, and do it now, Susan!"

"Copy that. Right away, Chief."

Chapter 12

Inside the van the four men no longer heard the sound of scratching and an uneasy calm came over them. Even the Chief who had just been on the radio noticed and turned his head in the direction of where the beast had been.

"It might be moving away," said Ben.

"But it hasn't flown away yet," Bob noted. "No rush of wind. We'll know if it flies because it'll kick up plenty of sand and dirt."

"Why do you suppose it's leaving?" the Chief asked.

"Sunrise. It's nocturnal," said Bob.

"Oh, yeah, you said that before. So, it doesn't waste any time and high tails it once the sun comes up?"

"Pretty much," said Bob, "but we have to be patient as it still might be lurking outside just out of sight waiting for us to come out."

"Are you telling me a creature like that can think?" the Chief asked with incredulity. "That it can set a trap for us?"

"It's a predator. Instinct. All creatures can draw upon millions of years of evolution when it's hunting."

A disgusted look crossed the Chief's face at the horrifying thought they could be food for the hideous creature. Simply contemplating the idea of being eaten alive was dreadfully gruesome. "But you think it'll be okay to go soon?"

"Yeah, soon but we'd best sit tight a bit longer," Ben cautioned, "until we're sure it's gone."

"I just can't believe something that big could be a bat! How could a bat attain such a size? I mean, what happened to it? How did it get so big? And where the hell did it come from?" asked the Chief, repeating his earlier questions.

"That's the essence of our assignment, Chief," said Ben. "We don't believe it came from around here or you'd have heard about them a lot sooner than now."

"Yeah, we think they migrated from somewhere," explained Bob, "but their origin is as yet unknown."

"So, you're certain there are more," the Chief stated, the question mark absent now.

"Oh, most assuredly so," said Ben.

"This is a lot more than we can handle," the Chief admitted. "I'll need to get in touch with the Governor to call out the National Guard...that is if he doesn't laugh me out of town. Who's gonna believe me?"

"We'll help with that," said Ben. "We've got that talon. There's nothing like the Federal Government to back up what you're saying. The governor will believe us."

Suddenly, they saw dust, and dirt and sand swirling into the air.

Bob peered out, "Yeah, it's flying away all right."

"The Chief and I will jump in his rover. Bob will go with Billy, so there'll be two of us in each vehicle...safer to travel in pairs if there is any trouble."

The Chief appreciated what Ben was saying so his son wouldn't be alone.

The Chief was about to exit, when Ben grabbed his arm to stop him. "Just to be on the safe side, let's assume the coast is not entirely clear. One of his pals might be lurking out there so we need to stay alert, move quickly and get into your vehicle immediately."

The Chief gulped. "I grew up with desert all around me...rattlers, scorpions, tarantulas, Gila monsters...but this is freaking me out," he wasn't ashamed to admit.

Ben nodded, "Yeah, you and me both."

Chapter 13

The two vehicles arrived in Sedona without incident and Chief Schmidt went to headquarters and directed his dispatcher, Susan, to call in all police personnel for an emergency meeting and organize sending of all available units throughout town to get people off the streets and to shelter in place.

With the police emergency declared, the necessary protocols were activated.

The Chief contacted the mayor and brought him up to date. The mayor in turn contacted the mayor of Phoenix and the mayors of its surrounding towns to alert them to the emergency.

The Sedona Performing Arts Center, the high school, middle schools and various other venues were open as shelters and per city protocols food and water was already being delivered to them via police escort.

It was the Police Chief with Ben on the speaker phone who notified the governor and requested the National Guard. Ben made the nature of the emergency clear and instructed the governor to advise the Guard that upon their arrival in Sedona to standby, and remain in their vehicles until they received their orders.

As Officer Billy Schmidt steered his patrol car up and down Main Street, every policeman and policewoman in Sedona was on duty stopping cars, closing the streets and escorting everyone inside into whatever building was nearest as all the restaurants and businesses as well as the schools would be utilized as shelters.

A couple finished an early breakfast and were peering out of the restaurant's window curious to see what was going on. Word there had already been received that everyone had to stay inside...that a lockdown of Sedona was in place.

"No one knows what it's all about. I'm thinking it's a possible terrorist attack," the woman commented.

"Maybe it's a crazed shooter that hasn't been apprehended," her husband ventured.

"I wish I knew what was going on."

"Yeah, me too, but whatever it is, it's serious. This is a tourist town. They wouldn't do something like this unless it was a dire emergency," he said, "but our motel is just down the block."

Officer Billy Schmidt spotted the man and his wife as they exited the restaurant.

Billy announced over his patrol car's loudspeaker, "This is a police emergency. Everyone must stay off the streets. Get back inside...now!"

"Our motel is a short walk down the street," the man shouted and pointed. "We'd better get moving," said the man, as he and his wife quickened their pace when a sudden rush of wind kicked up dirt and swirled into the air.

As they were crossing the intersection, one of the creatures appeared and leapt upon the woman's husband. The creature's sharp teeth tore into him and began lapping up the spurting blood as his wife looked on in horror.

Officer Schmidt reached for the twelve-gauge shotgun in his patrol car.

The man's wife screamed uncontrollably in terror as the beast preyed upon her husband while the creature appeared oblivious to both her and the approach of Officer Schmidt.

Billy quickly positioned himself between the woman and the creature just a few feet away and quickly saw there was no hope for the woman's husband.

"Help him!" the woman shouted.

As the creature stooped over on its haunches feeding ferociously, Billy leveled his shotgun and fired at point blank range. The monstrous abomination exploded in a bloody splatter as a pulp of muscle and sinew blasted a dozen feet into the air. A look of incredulity flashed across Billy's face as he stared at what remained of the creature.

Billy bent down and checked the woman's husband for a pulse. When he arose, he took the man's wife in his arms, and said, "I'm sorry. He's gone."

The woman wailed in her grief as Billy escorted her back into the restaurant.

"Please, you can't just leave him there like that," she wept.

Billy took her hands in his, and said, "I promise, I won't leave him there," said Billy.

When Billy returned to his patrol car, he called for two body bags.

Chapter 14

It was 8:15 a.m. at the police station when Chief Schmidt received a call. An aide on the other end of the line handed the phone to the governor who wanted an update after deploying the National Guard.

"They haven't arrived as yet, governor. We have one confirmed death that occurred this morning. The pilot and passenger from the downed plane are still missing."

"With those creatures out there, you may never find them," the governor stated.

"We haven't given up hope," said the Chief.

The governor caught himself in the midst of his pessimism, and replied, "Good, that's good," but soon returned to realism. "I want all of the Guard's resources scouring the state for those abominations."

"Understood, governor."

"I saw the pictures you sent of the dead creature. Any idea yet how many there are?"

"No information on that yet. We're all in beginning phase of this situation and we really don't have any information to go on except those photos and eye witness accounts."

"Do you have any idea where they're located...where they nest...I mean if there are more of them?"

"At this point we're trying to get all citizens inside to safety. We won't attempt a search and destroy operation until the National Guard arrives."

"Of course, of course, you'll need that manpower to take on a task such as that," the governor nodded at the other end of the phone. "The problem with being a Chief Executive is I rarely have real time information when I am not on site."

"As Chief of Police, I can't be everywhere either so I understand your frustration, sir."

"Of course, of course," the governor repeated.

"Can I be of further assistance Chief?"

"At the moment...,"

"Would it help for me to go to Sedona?"

"Not at this time governor because when the guard arrives, we'll deploy them shortly thereafter and it could very well be a combat situation when we find the creatures."

"I see, of course."

"The photo you received is one of the creatures that one of my officers killed."

"Where did that occur?"

"In the middle of town, I'm afraid."

"Damn! They're coming out of the desert?"

"At least one of them did...getting brazen I suppose, but it was very early in the morning."

"I don't follow."

"They're nocturnal. The thinking is that creature would have returned soon to wherever its colony is but it saw someone on the street and attacked."

"There shouldn't be anybody on the street," the governor raised his voice, "and what do you mean by a colony? How many are there of those creatures?"

"Again, we don't know how many. I'm told the most likely place where they'll be found is in the caves around Sedona that are large enough to accommodate such immense creatures. We'll start the search as soon as possible after the National Guard arrives."

"Where's that creature that was killed?" the governor asked.

"The remains were gathered up and sent over to the morgue to be put on ice until some biologist or the like can examine it to see if they can determine why it got so big."

"I'll get my staff to make several contacts and see who can get to Sedona on the double."

"That would be appreciated governor."

"Okay. I know it's a fluid situation but please keep me posted."

"I certainly shall, governor."

Chapter 15

Bob dozed in a chair at the police station when Professor Stephanie Lomax of Arizona State University approached Ben, and commented, "I understand you were injured by one of the fangs."

"One of its talons, actually," Ben smiled.

Bob opened his eyes to see a tall, slender woman with a shapely figure complimented by radiant green eyes. She was not the straightlaced professor Bob expected.

Ben saw Professor Lomax address Ben rather seductively, as she said, "Please excuse my appearance. I've been isolated in the lab for quite some time, and I was in the shower when I received the call. I left my place immediately. Afraid I didn't take the time to...,"

"You look fine," said Ben, as a grin on his face widened into a smile.

Bob saw it was obvious she was attracted to Ben. *God, she's everyman's dream, and she falls for Ben*, thought Bob in disbelief. *Why does Ben get the woman? Why isn't she attracted to me? What women don't fall for nice guys? She falls for a bastardo like Ben?*

Bob cleared his throat to be noticed in hopes of being introduced.

Ben eyed him, then turned back to the professor, and said, "He's coming down with a cold. You should probably steer clear of him."

"No, no, no! I don't have a cold!" Bob objected.

"Bob! Bob!" Ben shook him. "Wake up! Wake up!"

Slowly, Bob sat up in his chair...groggy."

"You were asleep," Ben stated, "and I believe you were having a conversation with yourself again."

"Huh?" Bob's eyes opened and darted back and forth nervously, "What?"

"You were talking out loud," Ben told him. "You were talking in your sleep."

"Oh," Bob replied, as he shook his head. "Is it any wonder with all the traveling we do in our assignments?"

"I know, I know," said Ben, "you're exhausted."

"Have the experts from Arizona State University arrived?"

"I don't know, why?" asked Ben.

"No one named Professor Stephanie Lomax?" Bob asked.

"Not as far as I know," Ben shook his head, and then grinned widely. "Oh, that's the name of the woman in your dream. Well, sorry pal, no sexy woman is on her way to Sedona."

Bob shook his head in disappointment, "You know, in the sci-fi movies they often send for an expert who turns out to be a good-looking woman."

"Yeah, they do, but we're not in a movie. Come on, before you hallucinate further."

Chief Schmidt was close enough to have heard it all, as he shook his head and returned to the matter at hand. "I sent photos of the evidence to the governor. He and his staff have been reviewing the information and in turn the information was sent to the National Guard so as to avoid delay in deployment. He gave the okay. I followed that with a phone call to Colonel Clayton of the Army National Guard. He heads up the Guard's Immediate Response Unit. Their motto is...always ready...always there. He said he'd be in Sedona with a contingent of the Guard within the hour."

Chapter 16

Glen pulled his Land Rover up to the curb in front of Pete's diner and stopped. He quickly scanned the immediate area, got out and walked around to the passenger's side of the car.

After Barbara exited the vehicle, Glen walked her to the door.

Barbara could see the concern in her husband's eyes, and said, "Hey, I'll be okay. Besides, I'm probably safer in town than alone at home, and people are going to get hungry while they're sheltering in place. Volunteers from our church are helping out in eateries all over town. That's why I called Pete so I could help him get meals prepared."

"Just be sure when a batch of food is ready you contact the police hot line for them to come get it...and you stay put inside! I don't want you out and about," Glen cautioned.

Barbara grinned, "You're not developing that anticipatory anxiety thing like that agent Bob has, are you?"

Glen shrugged, "With the enormous size of the creatures we're searching for I think I already have it."

"Well, I'm a big girl so don't worry, but I'm not about to hoof it alone to deliver meals," said Barbara, as she kissed her husband goodbye and entered the diner.

Chapter 17

As Ben, Bob and Chief Schmidt were wrapping up, Glen Armstrong arrived at police headquarters attired in his hiking outfit with gear in hand. "I'm ready to go when you are and I've got a list of the cave possibilities."

Glen handed the list to Ben who perused it and said, "Thanks for this, Glen. We want you to remain at police headquarters to answer any questions that might arise as we search the caves but under no circumstances are you to come along."

"But...,"

"Sorry, but this is a government operation. Absolutely no civilians allowed," said Ben, but upon seeing the disappointment on reflected on Glen's face, he added, "We need you on the radio to guide us. Will you help us?"

Glen hesitated, but relented, "Sure, of course. I'll help you in whatever way I can."

As soon as the National Guard's Immediate Response Unit arrived in Sedona, Colonel Clayton addressed one of his junior officers, "Captain, standby for my orders."

"Yes, sir."

Chief Schmidt, Colonel Clayton, Ben and Bob then huddled at police headquarters while Glen looked on.

After the introductions, Chief Schmidt asked, "You've been fully briefed?"

"I've been briefed...I don't know how fully. I still don't understand all of this," said Colonel Clayton, who was leading the unit.

"Don't feel bad; no one really understands any of this," said Chief Schmidt.

"Exactly how big are these bats?"

"Standing upright...ten feet tall."

"Whoa! How many are there?"

"We don't know."

"Well, let's just hope we find them," the colonel said gravely.

Colonel Clayton then directed a question to Ben, "As a special agent of the federal government, I assume you are in charge of this operation?"

"I am. Glen has provided us with the names of the caves that could accommodate these large creatures and we ran off several copies for your troops," he said, as he handed several of the lists to Colonel Clayton.

"We have the flame throwers you requested, and in addition to several tanks, we have a couple of flame throwing tanks. We've got everything you'll need," stated Colonel Clayton.

"Good," said Ben. "The guardsmen with the flame throwers come with us as well as a contingent with automatic weapons. The remainder of the Guard will need to stay to patrol Sedona to keep people off the streets and to take food and water as needed to those sheltering in place."

"Understood," replied Colonel Clayton, as he barked orders into his radio. "Flame throwers front and center."

"A cautionary note," said Ben, "your Guard needs to be in their vehicles as much as possible. These creatures are deadly and since they can fly they can attack from above and your people won't even hear them coming."

"Understood," the Colonel repeated, as he again barked orders into his radio.

"Okay, I think that does it. Let's get in our vehicles. Ben and Bob in the lead vehicle with me," said Chief Schmidt.

"I'm getting in the back of your rover with the agents as I may have some questions for them," said Colonel Clayton, as he handed one of his two-way radios to Glen. "My contingent of the Guard will follow us but that's in case you have to relay some specific directions to us."

"Okay," Glen spoke into the radio so that everyone involved in the operation could hear him. "You're going to head northwest. Your first stop will be Soldier Pass Cave. The cave is only about fifty meters in length but it could house a small colony of those creatures, and since we don't know how many of those creatures there might be...,"

"Yeah," Bob interjected, "it's best to err on the side of caution and check all the possibilities."

Chapter 18

As the caravan of vehicles rolled out of Sedona, helicopters loomed overhead on their way toward the nearby mountains where the search would begin for the enormous bats.

Though the overnight temperature dipped to sixty-four degrees, the mercury had already risen to eighty-nine degrees by 9:00 a.m. and was forecasted to go much higher as the day progressed.

While several tanks followed at a distance, the caravan neared the hills, slowed and stopped.

The occupants got out and ascended the hills on foot as a squad of infantrymen moved toward the entrance of the first cave.

On the outer parameter of the cave, the Colonel stationed several of his men...some with flame throwers and some with bazookas as well as a team of riflemen.

Ben and all the guardsmen had a helmet-mounted hands-free headlamp which lit up the cave and it didn't take long to determine Soldier Pass Cave did not have any of the creatures present.

Ben turned to Colonel Clayton, and said, "The creatures are nocturnal so if they're not here at this time of day, this is not their habitat."

Colonel Clayton asked, "Okay. Where to next?"

Ben checked the list. "We continue northwest to Subway Cave.

Glen, listening in at police headquarters, said, "Subway Cave is bigger. It goes back half a kilometer in length and in some places it's more than 5 1/3 meters high so it's certainly large enough to accommodate the creatures."

When silence ensued, Glen figured they were doing some calculating in their minds, so to save time, he clarified, "it's a third of a mile deep and up to seventeen feet high in places."

"Oh," several voices responded.

Glen muttered under his breath so no one could hear him, "Would be nice if you Americans got on the metric system."

When they arrived at Subway Cave and Colonel Clayton saw it was a steep climb, he turned to those he was traveling with, and stated unequivocally, "I don't want any of you going up there until we get armed men up there, so stay put down here until we get a contingent in place."

Chief Schmidt and Bob nodded their understanding and didn't argue, but Ben said, "I'm going up."

Colonel Clayton relented, "It's your expedition," as he turned, and said, "Captain, send a unit up but climb in pairs. If there are any of those creatures up there, I don't want our men picked off one by one. Have them cover each other."

"Yes, sir."

"When the first pair gets to the top, have them secure ropes over the side, so the rest of your command can get up there quickly," he ordered. "Ben here will be with the first pair."

"Yes, sir."

Three infantrymen approached the entrance, and Ben cautioned, "Be sure to check the ceiling as soon as you're in because they can attack from above."

One of the men gulped and swallowed hard.

Armed with automatic rifles affixed with flashlights on the barrels, the three infantrymen led the way as they crawled through the low, narrow, entrance of the cave and Ben followed behind them.

Outside, the remainder of the squad focused on the entrance and awaited the outcome. Some were armed with automatic rifles, others with flamethrowers. All of their weapons were aimed at the cave entrance ready to fire.

"Steady men. We've got people in there now. Nobody fires unless I give the command," Colonel Clayton alerted them. He then turned to Bob who was standing nearby, and said, "This might take a while, so what else can you tell me about these creatures?" as he was aware of Bob's reputation.

"Well, bats have changed very little over the last fifty million years. There are many different species, many varieties, and some bats survive for as long as thirty years, though we cannot know how long bats the size that we've seen can survive. They communicate and navigate with high-frequency sounds. Using sound alone, bats can detect everything but color.

"Normally, bats are very loyal to their birthplaces, but are capable of traveling vast distances. In their flight they have been timed at forty miles per hour and have reached heights of up to 10,000 feet. How fast, how high, and how far these large specimens can go is anybody's guess, but I believe it would be much less than a normal sized bat."

"Why is that?" the colonel inquired.

"Their size, weight. We think they migrated or at least began their migration when they were much smaller."

"Where do you think they originated?"

"Well, the smaller species of the enormous bats we've seen is commonly found in the south-central part of the United States...Kentucky, Tennessee. They navigate by radar in what is known as the echo location system, and it is quite literally millions of times more efficient than any system of radar developed by humans. In fact, their sense of sound is so acute they can detect obstacles as fine as a human hair. And, contrary to popular belief, bats are not blind. Many have excellent vision."

Colonel Clayton noted what Bob conveyed, and commented, "So, it would be very difficult to hit them via surprise attack. They could both see and hear us coming."

Bob nodded his confirmation.

"Why haven't they been seen until now?"

"Well, for one thing they hunt at night going out around sunset. Thus, they go unseen in the darkness. Secondly, they live in tree tops or in caves where they are not normally seen during the day. Since tree tops, could not support the weight of the bats we encountered, we believe they reside in caves during the day. Because I want you to understand exactly what we may be up against, colonel, a colony with normal sized bats located in Bracken Cave in Texas has more than fifteen million bats."

"Million! You did say million...fifteen million?" the colonel asked stunned as he stared with astonishment at the entrance of the cave his men had entered.

Bob nodded seriously.

Colonel Clayton then asked, "Are bats attracted to light?"

"The light draws the bats near because insects are attracted to the light and the bats eat the insects. They'll swarm around a street lamp to feed on insects but that's normal bats. Creatures the size we're searching for...well...they might come to the light to feed on us."

"Eyes sharp everyone!" shouted Colonel Clayton into his radio.

The flashlights of the infantrymen illuminated the cave unevenly with each step they took, and as they continued onward, the cave ceiling became lower and lower. They could not stand fully erect and stooped as they moved along slowly. It was slow going along a five-foot wide ledge as the narrow walkway and loose stones hindered their progress, but they continued to push forward and deeper into the damp, gloomy cave.

Forty-five minutes later the squad leader who was out front ordered, "Halt!" He reached for his radio, and reported, "It's not this one, colonel. We've reached the end of the cave. Nothing here. There are no other passages. We're coming out."

Colonel barked orders around the perimeter of the cave. "Stand down. At ease. They're coming out. Repeat, stand down."

Chapter 19

"Two caves down. What's next?" Colonel Clayton asked into his radio.

"Continue heading northwest toward Grand Canyon Caverns," stated Glen from police headquarters. "There's a new cave, unexplored. It's just off old route 66 a few miles before the Caverns after you pass the famous Burma Shave sign."

"What?" Ben asked. "What sign did you say?"

"You heard correctly. It's a Burma Shave sign. That's why it's famous...because it's still out there."

"Oh, okay, but what do you mean, it's a new cave?"

"Well, sometime after you pass the sign, look to your left. You'll see a large hole in the side of a hill. It wasn't there a couple of months ago. One day when I was returning from the Grand Canyon Caverns with a tour group it was suddenly there. I wanted to pull over to have a look but several in the group had to get back so we couldn't stop."

"Hmm, how big of a hole?"

"Big enough that you can see it from old route 66 even though that hill is a distance from the road. I'd estimate the hole is maybe as much as fifty meters across and perhaps ten meters high.

Ben nodded, "No wonder you could spot it from the road. That's a huge opening."

"There was a cave-in a number of months ago at an old silver...uh...no a copper mine, yeah, an old copper mine that's close by so maybe that had a hand in causing the opening. I marked it on the map as I figured you'd want to check it out," said Glen.

Back in Sedona, Officer Billy Schmidt drove his squad car down Main Street as he and other officers patrolled the town. Though they had their radios set on the frequency for police business in Sedona, they could all stay apprised of the situation by switching frequencies to that of the search party. Billy switched back and forth several times to hear if anything was happening.

When the search party approached the Burma Shave sign, Ben saw the opening in the side of the hill and directed them to turn and go off road. Because of the distances involved in the search party's first two stops, it was mid-afternoon when they reached the entrance of this new cave.

"Stay alert men," Colonel Clayton cautioned his troops. "We didn't see anything in the first two stops; that's when you tend to let your guard down. Don't!" he cautioned them.

"That's a big entrance," said Ben.

"Yeah, Glen was right on," said Bob, "and I'm coming with you this time."

"I'm going as well," Chief Schmidt stated. "No problem for my girth to get through that opening."

"What's that?" Bob asked, as he pointed to a sheath hanging from Ben's belt.

"Machete," Ben answered, "thought I'd bring it along in case I need it for close-in fighting."

Bob's eyes widened at the thought of being that close to those monsters to use a machete.

Colonel Clayton sent in additional troops as a contingent of twenty entered the cave. He had the remainder of his force take up positions outside covering the entrance.

As the search party proceeded into the cave it widened considerably.

Abruptly, Ben raised his hand for all to stop.

The squad leader and his men halted immediately.

Ben raised his index finger to his pursed lips to signal the others.

Ben listened closely and so did every man in the cave.

Nervously, Bob's eyes darted back and forth and upwards as he scanned the ceiling.

With Ben's keen sense of hearing, he heard something and he turned in the direction of the sound. He saw in the distance the steady drip of water from stalactites hanging overhead, water drop by drop dripping into puddles below.

Ben signaled them to move on as the numerous flashlights attached to twenty automatic rifles of the National Guardsmen illuminated the cave...again in ominous bouncing shadows with each step they took.

No more than five minutes later Ben raised his hand again as they approached another tunnel.

Bob leaned in, and said, "Yogi once said when you come to a fork in the road...take it."

"Good old, Yogi," Ben replied.

"Which one do you think is less traveled?" Bob asked.

"Hmm," Ben acknowledged, "I wonder if Frost would say the one less traveled would make all the difference here?"

"It very well may," Bob swallowed hard.

"I don't want us to split up. We'll take the right fork since it looks larger and might better accommodate those creatures. If it turns out to be a dead end, we'll return here and search the other tunnel."

"Sounds good," Bob agreed, as Ben signaled the search party they would take the right fork.

As Ben led the group to the right, he felt his footing become unsure. He signaled the group on the radio, "Be careful. The cave floor is uneven, so let's take it real slow and careful."

As they gradually proceeded, Bob commented, "I wish we had one of those sticks that mountain climbers use when they poke it into the snow to check for a firm footing."

"Just take a glance downward now and then. The helmet light will help and you'll see if we are walking on an irregular rock bed," Ben advised.

As they moved deeper into the tunnel, their footing became slippery and a pungent, musky smell assaulted their senses.

"This is it," Ben whispered.

"Yeah, that's the scent of bat guano," Bob replied.

"I always said you had a nose for crap," Ben quietly ribbed him.

"Really?" Bob asked rhetorically. "In the middle of this assignment you...,"

"Listen!" Ben whispered, as he abruptly held up his hand for the group to stop. "I heard something."

"What?" Bob asked in a hushed voice.

No one moved a muscle as every pair of ears listened intently for some kind of sound and every pair of eyes was on alert.

As they stood motionless, they heard it...a kind of slurping sound.

The squad leader aimed his rifle and the attached flashlight into the dim shadows in the direction of the sound. "Shine your lights toward the back of the cave—-straight ahead, men," he cautioned in a hushed voice.

Twenty lights immediately fixed on the spot directed by the beam of light from the squad leader.

What came into view revolted them...the grotesque sight of a half dozen bats. Each of the hideous creatures was large but not nearly as big as what had been seen previously. These were no more than three feet tall. The young bats were feeding on a cadaver of one of their own.

"My God!" voiced Chief Schmidt.

"Probably got injured in some way and they turned on it," Ben commented.

"This is the place all right," said Bob. "These smaller ones are their offspring. Bats give birth one at a time, so there's got to be fully grown females in here...adult males as well...and they won't be far from their young," Bob cautioned.

Chapter 20

While all eyes were fixed upon the scene at the back of the cave, an enormous creature loomed up in the shadowy darkness just a few feet away. It leapt upon one of the guardsmen who screamed in horror. The creature's razor-sharp teeth punctured the man's neck and instantly tore out his esophagus, his limp body falling to the ground.

One of the other men turned and fired. Quickly, the full contingent of the national guardsmen opened fire. A torrent of gunfire illuminated the cave as yellow/orangish light from the muzzles mingled with the white light from the mounted flashlights. As a steady cascade of automatic gunfire ripped into the creature, chunks of its flesh were torn from its torso and the creature was thrust backwards violently as it slammed against the cave wall.

Outside the cave, the gunfire could be heard. One of the guardsmen with a bazooka readied himself by taking a step forward but lost his footing on the loose gravel. As he slipped and fell, his bazooka discharged. A shell discharged at an upward angle toward the cave and exploded over the entrance causing rocks and dirt to cascade down the hillside. When the dust settled, the entrance to the cave was blocked. The search party was deep within the cave at the time of the explosion so no one was injured by the blast, but they were completely cut off from the outside.

"Dammit!" screamed Colonel Clayton as he raced toward the entrance. "Come on! Come on! We've got to get them out of there!" he shouted to the troops, and reached for his radio. "We need help!" yelled Colonel Clayton into the radio. "We've got a cave-in with people inside! We need every available man to clear the entrance!"

As the troops rushed forward and worked furiously to clear the debris, they could hear the muffled but distinct sound of gunfire from the troops inside.

In Sedona, Officer Billy Schmidt had been listening in at this particular time and heard the commotion over the radio. "This is Officer Schmidt in Sedona. Come in."

"This is Colonel Clayton. We've got people trapped inside one of the caves."

"Yes, colonel, I heard it all on the radio."

"You got any bulldozers, son?"

"I'll send them immediately but they're two hours out. How many are trapped inside?"

"About twenty of my men, the two federal agents and...uh...," Colonel Clayton hesitated, as he realized who was on the radio.

"Is my dad in the cave?"

"I'm afraid so, but we can hear the sound of gunfire. We'll get them out, son. Just hurry up with that bulldozer!"

With siren blaring, Billy Schmidt pushed his foot to the floor and hurried toward the airport barking orders on his radio as he sped away.

Inside the cave, the flash from automatic rifles illuminated the darkened cave in sporadic bursts while the flashlights mounted on the rifles created an eerie scene of light beams abruptly moving from one target to another like an erratic laser show.

"Don't let the creatures flank us! Form a circle!" yelled the squad leader, as they continued to fire their weapons as more of the monstrous creatures appeared.

"Don't let them close in on us!"

"Watch out for their teeth!"

"Stay away from their claws!"

Another National Guardsman screamed as one of the creatures dug its teeth into the man's arm and dragged him several feet away. Then its razor-sharp teeth penetrated the man's neck puncturing his jugular, blood gushing from the wound.

Chief Schmidt fired at the beast. Bullets tore into the creature's head and splattered it to bits. He then fired at another of the onrushing monsters at point blank range killing it in its tracks. When another one of the creatures closed in on Chief Schmidt's blind side, Ben pulled out his machete and swept the blade across the creature's neck beheading it instantly...the spurting blood pulsing upward while the headless torso fell limply to the cave floor.

"Ben! The cave-in! We're enclosed!" Bob shouted.

Ben knew immediately the danger Bob alluded to. "All flame throwers cease! All flame throwers cease!" he commanded to conserve the oxygen in the now sealed cave.

"Fire arms only! Firearms only!" Ben commanded, as he spotted a large indent along the right side of cave wall.

"Grab the wounded! Everyone this way!" Ben shouted, as he led the troops to a low-ceilinged, U-shaped section of the cave.

There the creatures couldn't get at them from above, behind or from either side. The contingent of guardsmen with their backs to the wall fired at the continuous onslaught of the attacking creatures.

A steady stream of bullets tore into the hideous creatures. Shards of bat flesh exploded from their torsos dropping them in death to the cave floor amongst other bats crawling toward their prey. Guardsmen strafed those on the ground slamming them backwards in a flood of lethal rifle fire.

Suddenly, the attack stopped.

"Cease fire!" Ben directed the contingent.

With the cessation of gunfire, the moans of those wounded could be heard while the smell of blood permeated the chamber.

"Tend to the wounded. Bandage them up as best you can but stay alert," Ben cautioned. "Be on the ready for another attack and check your ammunition."

Officer Billy Schmidt screeched his car to a skidding stop at the Sedona airport and signaled the helicopter pilot he had contacted while enroute.

As Billy climbed in, he pointed to a spot on the map south of the Grand Canyon Caverns, and asked, "How soon can you get me there?"

"I'll push it. Hang on," he said, as the copter lifted off.

Chapter 21

Thirty-five minutes had elapsed before Billy Schmidt arrived on the scene by copter and ran to the entrance to join the others in working feverishly to remove debris from the entrance.

It was fully an hour and half later before bulldozers arrived via flat-bed as Billy and the others stepped back while the earthmovers began clearing the remainder of the rubble.

Inside, Ben and Bob stood shoulder to shoulder with the National Guard. The duo fired their Glocks in an effort to keep the creatures at bay as another wave of them attacked.

Chief Schmidt turned and saw the flickers of light beams approaching, and hollered, "They're in!"

Quickly, the squad leader notified the reinforcements of their position in the cave so as not to be in the line of fire.

"Stop at the fork!" Ben yelled into the radio. "We will meet you at the fork! Do not shoot! We are coming to you!"

The man in charge of the second wave of guardsmen directed his squad to hold their fire, but he ignored the order to stay in place as he ordered his troops forward toward the trapped contingent.

Ben directed everyone to move out of the U-shaped indent but to stay as close as possible to the side wall as they returned the same way they entered the tunnel.

There were fewer creatures attacking as the group moved along the wall and fired into the recesses of the tunnel to cover their retreat.

The second contingent of guardsmen arrived and Ben's face reflected his elation at seeing the additional guardsmen. Ben acknowledged such to the squad leader who commanded his troops to open fire at the oncoming creatures just as another wave of bats attacked.

Billy Schmidt, upon seeing that his father was not injured, rushed to the side of the wounded to help.

The Guardsmen with the flamethrowers stepped to the front and commenced firing. High-pitched squeals of the creatures echoed throughout the cave, as the flamethrowers charred the monstrous bats.

The far end of the cave was awash in flames as the search party and the reinforcements retreated hurriedly toward the entrance. The guardsmen moved backwards toward the entrance while continuing to fire their flamethrowers.

Once everyone was out of the cave, a flame-throwing tank now on site opened fire. A long band of yellow flame shot through the much-diminished entranceway into the inner reaches of the cave. None of the bats could challenge the searing heat of the flames, while Colonel Clayton directed the tank commander to continue firing, "Don't let up for a second!"

He then contacted his own helicopter pilot on site. "Aim your missiles for the opening of the cave. We want them to explode on the inside and bring the whole damn mountain down on the bastards!"

The tank continued to fire its stream of flame until commanded to back away from the entrance. When the tank ceased fire and was sufficiently clear, Colonel Clayton commanded the pilot, "Lock your missiles and fire when ready!"

The helicopter descended, hovered at the entrance and fired two missiles that rocketed into the bowels of the cave.

As the helicopter peeled away an enormous explosion sounded and a fireball flashed out of the entrance. The cave collapsed as tons of rock and dirt cascaded down on the remaining creatures inside, while a cloud of dust billowed out and upward from the entrance obscuring the scene.

For what seemed an eternity, everyone stood in silence...frozen in a blank stare.

When the dust finally cleared, the cave was sealed with debris.

"Well, that does it. Nothin' could live through that," Colonel Clayton commented confidently, as he moved off with the guardsmen.

As Chief Schmidt and Billy approached Ben and Bob, the Chief said, "We got the bastards!"

"Fried them and buried them," said one of the National Guardsmen.

Ben looked on but without elation. Neither was Bob overjoyed.

Chief Schmidt noticed and yelled, "What's the matter with the both of you!? We got 'em! We got 'em!"

The seriousness of the situation was reflected on Ben's face, as he replied, "Even if they're all dead, we don't know where they originated—-we can only narrow it to a general area of the country—-maybe—-and we don't know if there's more on the way. We don't even know why they grew to be so enormous," he reflected, and added, "We really don't know much about them at all."

Though Chief Schmidt remained convinced the creatures were destroyed, his elation ebbed as he pondered Ben's comments.

"There's still hope," Bob stated. "Though I certainly don't want to celebrate prematurely, on the bright side I'm working the physics of it. We're in the process of tracking them all down. We'll get them...eventually."

Sunset was only a few minutes away, and as darkness began to descend upon the desert, Ben spotted a swarm of the man-eating bats approaching...no doubt from one of the many other caves.

"No, no, no," Chief Schmidt shouted as if refusing to believe there were more of them. "My, God! There are hundreds of them!"

"Bob! The SRN system!" Ben yelled urgently!

Bob looked up, and as he ran to the truck, he shouted, "The Sound Reverberation Navigation System may not be large enough."

"We don't have a choice!" Ben yelled.

Bob jumped onto the truck, got to the SRN system, grabbed the pull cord and yanked with a mighty tug.

Nothing.

As the bats neared Bob gave it another hard pull.

Nothing again, as the creatures were nearly overhead.

"It needs air!" Ben yelled. "Hit the primer pump!"

"Always the supervising critic telling me how to do something," Bob muttered under his breath, as he pushed the pump button several times and grabbed the pull cord.

Ben checked the sky, and shot a quick glance back to Bob. "You've gotta do it now, Buddy. Come on! One time," Ben exhorted.

Bob yanked it abruptly and it revved up.

"All right!" Ben hollered in enthusiasm and pumped his fist in the air.

Bob pointed the mechanism's finder toward the oncoming creatures, which were now only seconds away.

The SRN was at a higher pitch than the human ear could detect, but it reverberated at a level that drove the enormous bats into madness instantly. The hideous creatures lost their sense of direction and their echo system of navigation failed immediately. The enormous bats plunged head first to earth. They hit the terrain at top speed in a tangled swarm of torsos, wings and claws and splattered against the desert floor...the impact spurting blood and guts into the air.

Not a single bat survived activation of the SRN system.

Chapter 22

With everyone breathing easier, Colonel Clayton approached Ben and Bob. "Gentlemen, you are to be congratulated. I thought for sure we were all bat bait when they dove at us."

"It certainly was close," Ben acknowledged.

"Just what exactly is that contraption of yours?"

"Well, it's a bit technical," said Bob, "but it was a little something I put together. Actually, Ben deserves all the credit. I built it, but it was per the specifications Ben provided."

"That's very generous of you, partner," Ben acknowledged, "but you might win another Nobel prize for inventing the SRN."

"Well, good job, gentlemen," said the colonel, and asked, "But why didn't you bring that SRN system into the cave?"

"Wouldn't have worked in a confined area," said Bob, "it's only good out in the open."

The colonel nodded his understanding. "Well, once again, a job well done, gentlemen," and headed back to rejoin his troops.

The Chief and Billy Schmidt approached the duo as Bob began to rant at Ben. "You know, maybe you'll be a little more open with me in the future and tell me up front more of what is going on and not waiting until the last minute," he complained, and then muttered mockingly paraphrasing what Ben had said earlier to him, "North, we're driving north...just up the road...we're going camping...I always wanted to go camping."

Ben chuckled.

"What a bunch of crap!" said Bob.

Chief Schmidt interrupted Bob's rant by clearing his throat, and stating, "Uh, just wanted to say thanks to both of you."

"Yes, thanks," Billy echoed, "we are indebted to you."

"Well, you're welcome," said Ben.

"Just doing our job," said Bob.

Ben noticed that the Chief appeared somewhat distracted, alone in his thoughts.

"Chief?" Ben enquired.

"Huh?"

"You okay?"

"Oh, I was just thinking about what you said earlier. I'm worried about the people of Sedona. You really don't think we got them all?"

"Oh, we got all the ones that were here," Ben confirmed.

"But you think there are others around the country?"

"I don't think there's any doubt that other sightings will be occurring but we're better off now than we were. We've got the SRN and we've confirmed that it works."

"Yeah," Bob interjected, "now that we've confirmed its operation we can get the SRN into production and send them to communities around the country."

The Chief's eyebrow arose, "It's that serious, huh?"

"Not sure," Ben nodded, "but we've got alerts out to law enforcement. We are certainly in a much better position now than we were just twenty-four hours ago."

"Do you think we'll ever know why they got that way? Why they grew so large?" Billy Schmidt asked.

Ben pursed his lips, and shrugged. "I don't know. Maybe the bat cadaver we have on ice in Sedona will tell us something," Ben suggested, as he glanced at the heap of carcasses on the hillside, and added, "Maybe there's enough left of these to study. But we'll see. We'll get the chemists going on the blood work and tissue samples. Perhaps they'll be able to give us some answers. Afterall, science has been known to learn things about the world in which we live."

"Well, I sure hope they can learn something about those grotesque monsters," mused Chief Schmidt.

"Good luck to you both," Ben offered, as the duo shook hands with the Schmidts, and Ben added, "We'll certainly be in touch if anything happens or if we receive any additional news."

"And believe me, if we have another incident, you'll be the first ones we call," the Chief chuckled.

As Ben and Bob headed for the truck that would take them back to Sedona, Ben asked, "How's it going with that tracking device you developed?"

"We should know by tomorrow...if I perfected it," said Bob.

"What's the principle behind it?"

"Bats operate by sonar. When they do, they emit a chemical in trace amounts that leaves a tract...an invisible, narrow swathe that remains for weeks or longer as it descends to the ground," Bob explained.

"And the gadget you developed picks up that chemical?"

Bob nodded, "Hopefully, and follows it all the way back to where it originated."

"Well, if it works and you actually can track them to their point of origin, get ready to slap a name to it because you could very well win two Nobel prizes," Ben grinned widely.

Epilogue

The next morning over coffee at the Phoenix airport, Ben and Bob were watching the news as they awaited their flight.

"It was nice of the Armstrongs to fix us breakfast before we departed," Ben commented.

"Yeah, it was a very nice gesture," Bob agreed, "especially after Glen was disappointed that he wasn't allowed to join us searching the caves. Of course, I would have preferred to sleep in a bit longer. Those six a.m. breakfasts, whew! I don't know how they do that."

"Ah well, we had to be up for our flight anyway," said Ben.

"Yeah," Bob acknowledged, as he elbowed Ben seated beside him at the counter.

"Yeah, I see," said Ben, eyeing the television screen thinking Bob was referring to a news story.

"No, no, I mean you never said...,"

"What?" asked Ben, as he took a sip of his coffee.

"Which animal would you come back as if you had to pick one?"

"Huh?" Ben wondered what Bob was talking about.

"Remember? I said if I had to come back, I'd be a hippopotamus because no one messes with a hippo."

"Oh," Ben nodded as he now recalled.

"What would you pick?" Bob asked.

Ben thought for a moment, and replied, "I think any flying bird would be fine with me."

Unable to restrain himself, Bob took the bait. "Why would you want to be a bird?"

"Well, you know, the freedom of flight. To fly around like a bird would be exhilarating. And it would have the added bonus of being able to hover over you and drop my offerings on your head," Ben replied with a straight face.

"Yeah, yeah, real funny," Bob replied, as he now noticed a news story.

Bob motioned to the man behind the counter, "Hey, would you mind turning up the volume on the television?"

"No problem," as he grabbed the remote.

As the news story came across the screen, Ben and Bob both straightened up in their seats when an image of Mammoth Cave appeared on the television.

The news broadcaster reported, "The U.S. Department of Interior announced today the closing of historic Mammoth Cave in Kentucky. Army Engineers were sent in during the night to seal off the entrance. Clyde Mathews, Secretary of Interior, stated that the popular tourist attraction has been closed until further notice for safety reasons due to unsafe conditions within the cave. He offered no further details. In an unrelated story, information is still sketchy about a strange occurrence in and around the picturesque city of Sedona, Arizona."

Ben and Bob eyed each other knowingly as they picked up their respective carryon bag and headed for the departure gate.

Other Ben & Bob Adventures

The Pantheon Hotel
Prisoners of Paris
Beware Sundown
In the Land of Eternal Spring
Nostradamus: The First Prophecy
Ghost Shack
Piazza Navona
Purple Mountain Majesties
Discovery
Windy City Terror